For the little monsters: Zoe, Kieran, Alexander, and Edward   M.R.

For Lidia   S.H.

Text by Mark Robinson
Illustrations copyright © 2010 Sarah Horne
This edition copyright © 2010 Lion Hudson

The moral rights of the author and illustrator
have been asserted

A Lion Children's Book
an imprint of
Lion Hudson plc
Wilkinson House, Jordan Hill Road, Oxford OX2 8DR
www.lionhudson.com
Paperback ISBN 978 0 7459 6167 5
Hardback ISBN 978 0 7459 6254 2

First UK edition 2010
1 3 5 7 9 10 8 6 4 2 0
First US edition 2010
1 3 5 7 9 10 8 6 4 2 0

A catalogue record for this book is available
from the British Library

Typeset in 17/22 Tempus Sans ITC
Printed in China May 2010 (manufacturer LH06)

Distributed by:
UK: Marston Book Services Ltd, PO Box 269, Abingdon, Oxon OX14 4YN
USA: Trafalgar Square Publishing, 814 N Franklin Street, Chicago, IL 60610

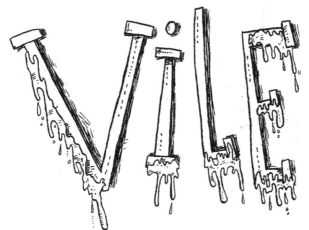

A Cautionary Tale for Little Monsters

Mark Robinson – Sarah Horne

LION
CHILDREN'S

A brand-new term is starting in the town of Beastieville.
The ancient School of Manners stands there, high upon a hill.
The friendly monsters go there, as suits their talents best,
  all smiling, bright, and eager-eyed.
    But as for all the rest…

... For those who pester, pinch, and push,
who sniffle in their snot;
the University of Vile awaits this monstrous lot.

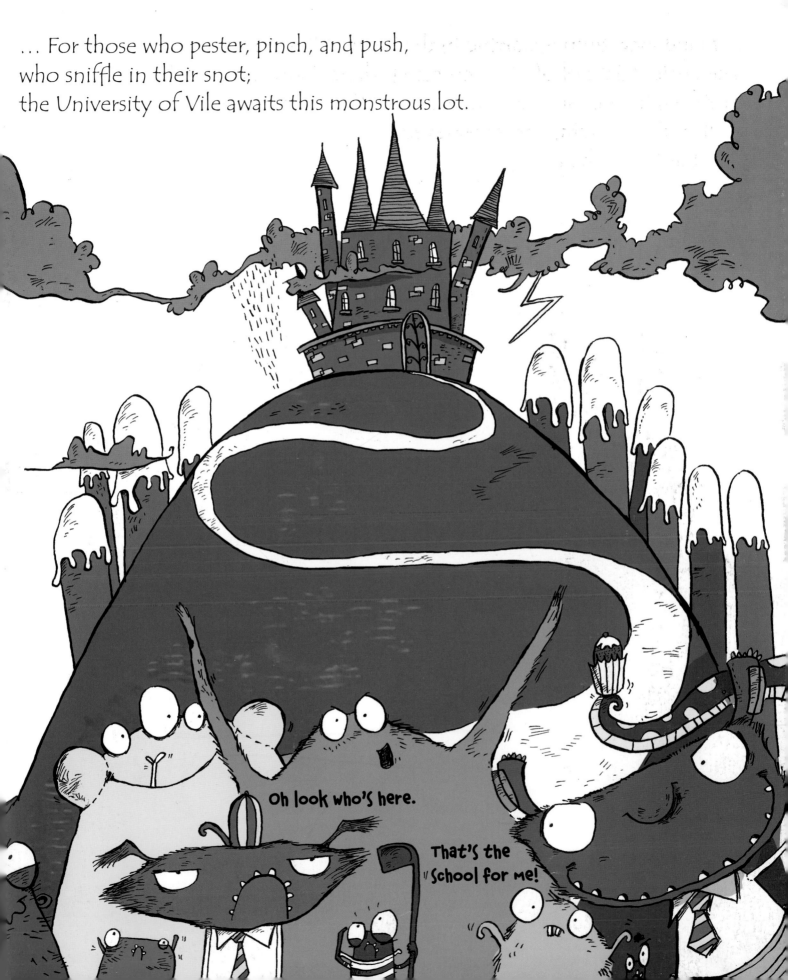

For here they get encouragement to reach their true potential,
where naughtiness and mischief – and rudeness – are essential.
They have to say how bad they've been when they arrive each day,
so tripping, teasing, trumping must be tried along the way.

It's vital in the classroom to be messy, loud, and spiteful.
"More volume, class," the teacher calls.
"A racket is delightful."

When midday comes, so much to learn: what makes a lousy lunch?
What kinds of gloopy, greasy things should monsters love
  to munch?
Why is it quite so vital that one always plays with food?
And why burp loudly all the time?
(Well, not to would be rude!)

In Science classes no one may wear goggles or take care.
Explosions, stinks, and toxic gas completely fill the air.

A heatproof mat? Well, who needs that?
It's not that kind of school.
"To be as vile as possible!"
That is the golden rule.

Then off outside to play some sports and be extremely mean,
inflicting pain on *everyone*, not just the other team.

When school is done, the monsters all are keen to be away.
Just see how fast they shoot off home, for yet more work and play.

There's chores to do, and pets to scare,
   and dirt to trample in,
upending rooms, unmaking beds...
   the usual kind of thing.

Then one day, after playing out and monkeying around,
two monster enemies both saw a big hole in the ground.

To be the first to take a look, they pushed and shoved about.
One played a trick, but both fell down...

Oh no! Beware! Look out!

Deep in the hole was damp and gloomy, murky, dark, and vile... and those most fiendish monsters soon began to lose their smile.

Stuck and stranded, tired and bored, and knowing it was late,

they could see just one way out: they must *cooperate!*

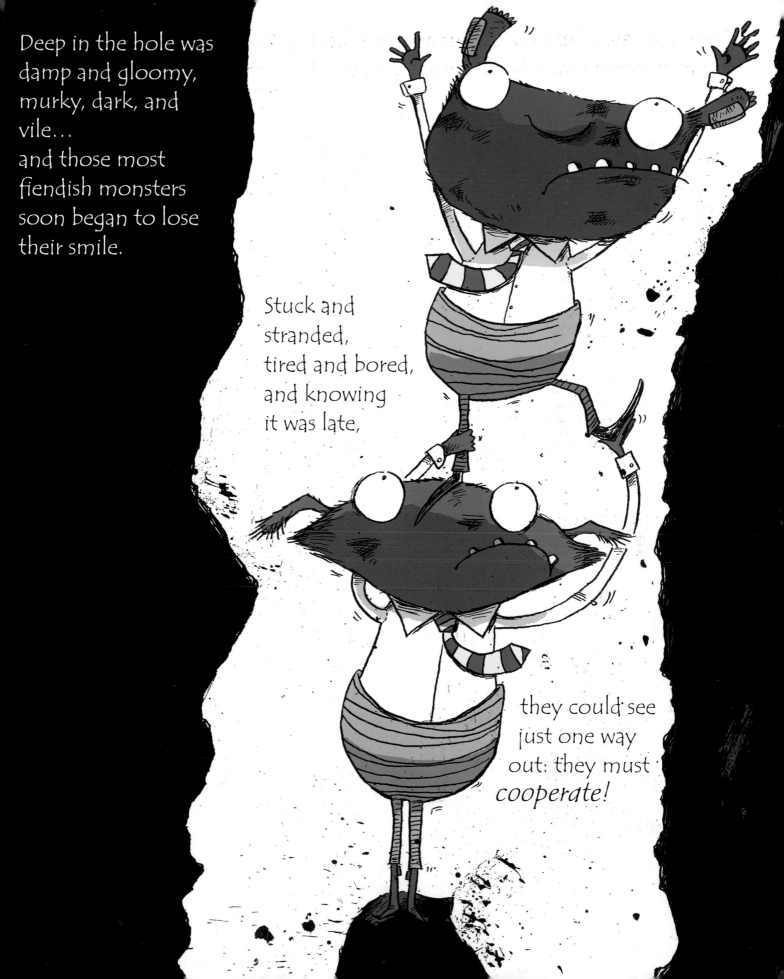

There were whispered stories in the corridors next day:
a shocking tale of friendship – just what would the teacher say?

The Head – he went bananas! No one knows how he found out.
He called the pair before him and at once began to shout:
"You've let the whole school down with this! Do you not understand?
Your goodness is against school rules: you're permanently banned."

The little School of Manners has a very different style,
which suited those poor monsters who no longer acted vile.
Their teacher helped them learn to make right choices every day.
It felt a bit unusual – but really quite OK.

So now the term is ending in the town of Beastieville.
How are our little monsters in their new school on the hill?
They're smiling, bright, and eager-eyed, as you can clearly see.
But are they little monsters still?

Of course not!

It's best when everyone plays ball.

The end

(of the University of Vile, anyway)

Other titles from Lion Children's Books

Just Because   *Rebecca Elliott*
The Three Billy Goats' Stuff   *Bob Hartman & Jacqueline East*
The Wolf Who Cried Boy   *Bob Hartman & Tim Raglin*